Habie
The Hope Bear

To: Jilli
Pamela A. Erickson
Jan '08

Jayne Hanson and Sheila Dokken

Illustrated by Pamela A. Erickson

ISBN 10: 1-59298-208-5
ISBN 13: 978-1-59298-208-0
Library of Congress Catalog Number: 2007935850

Design/layout by Jill Blumer
Printed in Canada
First Printing: October 2007

11   10   09   08   07   5   4   3   2   1

Beaver's Pond Press

7104 Ohms Lane
Suite 216
Edina, MN 55439-2129
(952) 829-8818
www.BeaversPondPress.com

To order, visit www.BookHouseFulfillment.com or call 1-800-901-3480.
Reseller discounts available.

Teaching guides and study tools are available by calling 763-689-1804.

Dear Parents,

Hobie the Hope Bear came to life shortly after the devastation of 9/11. My children were very young at the time, and I was inspired to do something to make their future a better place. I've practiced discrimination law for several years, but quickly learned that it does not eliminate our prejudices. The law does not reach our hearts or touch our souls. Rather, our children are the key to achieving true understanding.

Children adopt the attitudes and beliefs they see and hear around them. When children are the victims of intolerance, their future is tainted, and the experience may color their attitudes and actions for the rest of their lives. As parents and teachers, these things are very difficult to talk about with our children. We can all use a little help in fighting to hold on to the innocence of our youngest children.

Hobie provides a promise for the future, a symbol of what life can be and what yet needs to be achieved. Despite all of our differences, we are first and foremost human beings. To achieve peace, we need to move beyond our prejudices to a new world of hope, love and compassion. It starts with our kids. Hobie will always be there for them and for you.

—Sheila Dokken

**For the love of our children,
who inspire us every day to make a difference.**

Danielle and Deanna
Allison, Amanda, and Kate
Penny and Barr

Sheila, Jayne, and Pamela

Hobie looked around the room and did not see one familiar face. He had been so excited for the first day of school, but now he felt a little scared and a little lonely. This was going to be a long year.

"Hobie, welcome to our classroom!" said Mrs. Honeypot, his new teacher.

"I am so excited about beginning a year of learning new and wonderful things, aren't you?"

"I guess so," Hobie mumbled.

Hobie glanced at the others in the room. No one looked like he did. Everyone was either taller, smaller, or a different color. How was he going to make friends when everyone was so different?

Hobie started drawing at his desk before class. His classmates talked about their summers and what games to play at recess. More students joined in the conversation, and no one seemed to notice Hobie. He felt a little left out.

Hobie spent so much of the day worrying about how he was different from everyone that he didn't talk to anyone new.

He ate lunch alone,

he played alone at recess,

and he even sat by himself during storytime.

When the others tried to include him in a game,

he just acted bashful and walked away.

At the end of the day, Mrs. Honeypot gave each of them a project to do at home. They were asked to make a poster about themselves.

The poster had to list five things that made each one of them special.

"This will be easy," Hobie thought. "I love to do so many things. The hard part will be to decide which five to choose."

"How was your first day?" asked Hobie's mom.

"Oh, it was okay," said Hobie.

"You don't sound very happy," replied his mom.

"I forgot my backpack," Hobie told her.

Noticing Hobie's sadness, Mom asked, "Is there anything else?"

"I don't know anybody, Mom."

"Didn't you make any new friends?" she asked.

"Well, no," said Hobie, not wanting to look her in the eye.

"Why not?" his mom questioned softly.

After thinking about it, Hobie said, "They are just so different than I am. No one looks like me. No one talks like me. No one is going to like what I like."

"Put your hand on your heart, Hobie. Your heart will help you remember that we shouldn't judge people by how they look on the outside. You'll be surprised how much we're all alike on the inside."

"All right, Mom, I will try harder," Hobie said, not feeling very sure that her advice would work.

After supper, Hobie cleared his place at the table and went to work on his poster. He had finally decided what he was going to put on his special list.

He was quite proud of his poster. He even drew little pictures next to each one. This project was turning out to be so much fun!

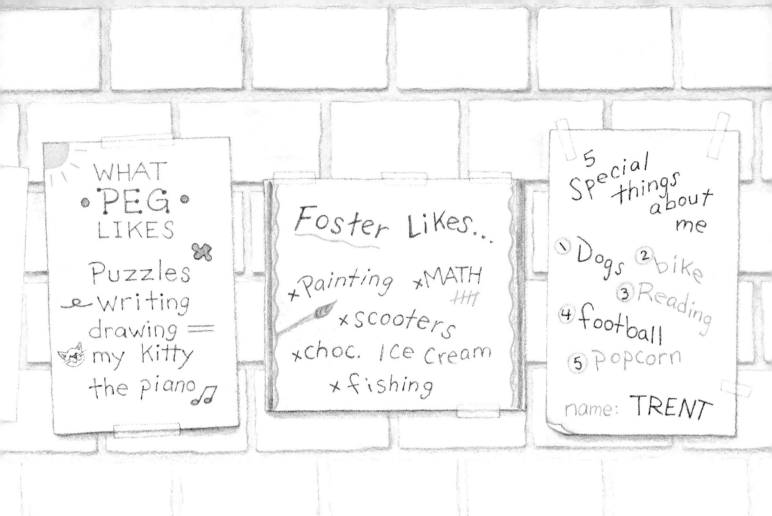

When Hobie arrived at school the next morning, many of the students had already hung up their posters. It was fun to see all of the different colors and designs.

Hobie hung his poster on the wall, next to the others, then backed up to take a look. At that moment, he noticed something amazing. Each student had written something that matched his poster. Hobie could not believe it. He put his hand to his beating heart.

Could everyone in his class, even though they seemed so different, be alike in some ways?

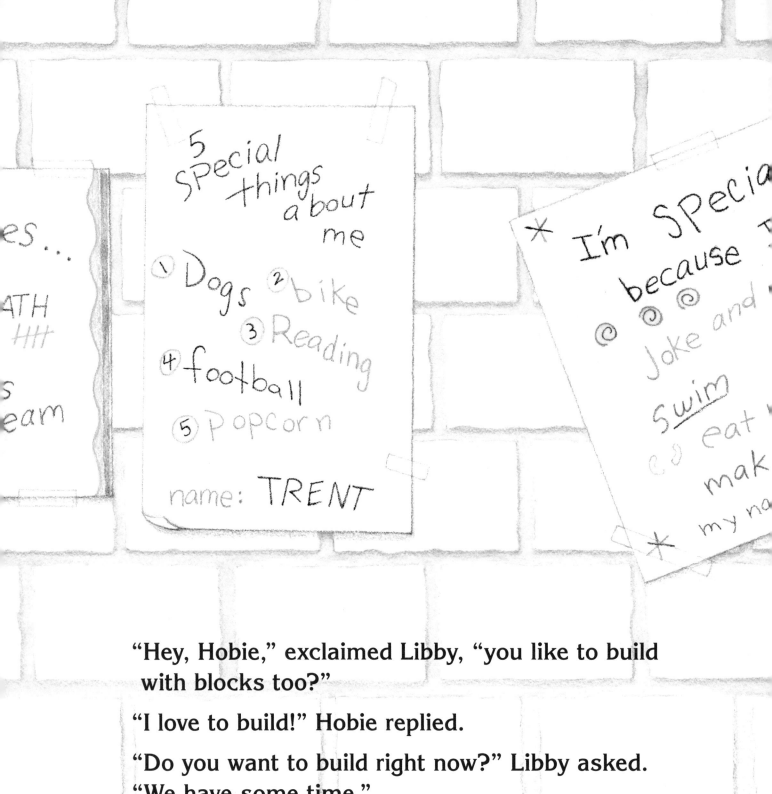

"Hey, Hobie," exclaimed Libby, "you like to build with blocks too?"

"I love to build!" Hobie replied.

"Do you want to build right now?" Libby asked. "We have some time."

"You bet!" said Hobie.

Hobie and Libby built a castle until
Mrs. Honeypot was ready to start class.

"Thanks for playing," said Hobie.

Libby smiled. "It was a lot of fun!"

Later that day, Mrs. Honeypot asked everyone to partner up and read a book together.

"Hey, Trent, how about being partners?" asked Hobie. "I saw on your poster that you like to read, too."

"Sure!" said Trent.

Then they sat down and read a story about
two tiger cubs that become very good friends.
It was a great story, and they had fun taking
turns reading.

During lunch, Libby and Trent asked Hobie to eat at their table. Hobie was glad to join in.

They sat around the table telling jokes and laughing.
There was even chocolate ice cream for dessert!

At the end of the day, Hobie and all of his
classmates lined up for their class picture.
As Hobie stood in line with his new friends,
he put his hand on his heart for just a second.
Mom had been right. From now on, Hobie
would not judge people by how they looked
on the outside.

MRS. HONEYPOT

HOPE ELEMENTARY

Hobie would always follow his heart.

THE  END

AUTHOR

Jayne Hanson has been an elementary school teacher since 1990. As a teacher, she has been writing curriculum, telling and creating stories for children, and finding new ways to connect with young people. She believes that children are the positive lights of the future that need to be cherished every day. Jayne lives with her husband and three children in Cambridge, Minnesota.

ILLUSTRATOR

Pamela A. Erickson landed her first freelance art job at the age of 17. She studied commercial and fine art. Pam worked in advertising layout/design and illustration, which led her to a 10-year career as an art director for a publishing company. Now enjoying the finer side of art, she currently works out of her studio in Elk River, Minnesota. Pam loved children's books as a child and appreciates them even more today. She lives with her husband and two children.

CREATOR

Sheila Dokken has been a discrimination attorney since 1993. Because of this experience, she has seen firsthand the destructive force of prejudice in our society. After realizing that proactive approaches are a far better alternative than the

legal system, she has been transitioning her practice into mediation and helping employers reduce the risk of employee lawsuits through training. She was inspired to do something positive to make a difference in the lives of children, thus leading her to develop the concept of Hobie the Hope Bear™. Sheila has a passion for children and is motivated to make a difference in their lives. She lives with her husband and two children in Elk River, Minnesota.